101 Things to Do on a Deserted Island

101 Things to Do on a Deserted Island

Patricia E. Snyder

Gamma Griz LLC

Paperback ISBN: 979-8-9909154-3-5
Ebook ISBN: 979-8-9909154-2-8

Gamma Griz LLC
132 NW 6th Street #1102
Grants Pass, OR 97526

www.GammaGriz.com

First Printing, 2024

Disclaimer

Use of this book implies acceptance of this disclaimer. Under no
circumstances will any blame or legal responsibility be held against
the publisher or author for any damages, reparation, or monetary loss
due to the information contained within this book, either directly or
indirectly, including, but not limited to, errors, omissions,
inaccuracies, or strandings. The information contained within this
book is for educational and entertainment purposes only. No
warranties of any kind are declared or implied, especially as it relates
to survival on, enjoyment of, or escape from a deserted island.
Readers acknowledge that the author is not engaged in the rendering
of legal, financial, medical, professional, or survival advice. Consult a
professional before attempting any techniques described in this book.
This book contains references to fiction and nonfiction sources, and
inclusion in no way implies affliation with, or endorsement of, source
material, individuals, or companies on the part of the author or
publisher.

Statement of Human Creativity

No artificial intelligence was used in the creation of this material.
Patricia Snyder toiled for hours over the words and illustrations, on
top of all of the time spent digging into island myths, legends, books,
movies, and television series, her lips dry from all the salty popcorn
and hands sore from holding heavy books and playing video games.
Her effort to bring you this work is not unlike the vulnerable young
penguin who endures the chill of being born in Antarctica, only to
trek unimaginable distances to the ocean. Years — nay, decades—
passed as this simmered inside her human intelligence until it fought
its way up through the publishing process. Let us take a deep breath
together. Doesn't that feel good?

So It Begins

You survived the crash, or the storm, or the magical whirlwind, or some quirk of fate, and now you find yourself stranded on a deserted island. Congratulations! You have this handy book of things to do. There's no need for actionless wandering, lollygagging, or directionless bumbling about. You can now bumble with purpose.

~1~

Confirm you are, in fact, on an island.

As ancient tales alert us, some places are actually very large creatures upon whom plants have grown. If you instead are stranded on a very large whale, turtle, seahorse, or other being, please close this book and refer to the appropriate reference guide.

~2~

Ponder etymology.

As you peer about your new home, contemplate whether it is a *desert island* or a *deserted island* and reflect on the study of word origin, etymology. Consider how, hundreds of years ago, the Latin word *desertus* meant abandoned. Yes, you are on a desert isle, abandoned, or as you might say, a deserted island. Feel smug about your word choice, either way.

~3~
Make a *sand*wich.

Other delicious foods associated with deserted islands include rocky road ice cream, mud pies, and grits.

Recipe for Deserted Island Hot Dogs
1. Obtain and cook hot dogs.
2. Put on bun, no bun if keto.
3. Add condiments.
4. Eat on a deserted island.

~4~
Dig in!

If you have been fortunate enough to be stranded on a *dessert* island, you will appreciate the easily harvestable array of desserts. Enjoy Island Pie, Ocean Cake, and Atlantic Beach Pie, but don't forget to first eat your vegetables. Finish your salad with Thousand Island dressing.

~5~
Look for water.

Once the haze of your island feast wears off, you're sure to be thirsty. Survival guidance says that drinking seawater just dehydrates you more, which doesn't make sense because it's water, right? Still, listen to the "scientists" and "medical experts" about this and look for the unsalty kind. Sparkling, if you prefer.

If you don't want to trust your gut…
Near so much ocean water, your parched lips may call for a drink. If you're one of those thinky-type people, the American Museum of Natural History's Ask a Scientist website feature (look it up if your island has Wi-Fi) claims that ocean water has so much salt that your kidneys need more water to remove the salt from your blood than comes with the salty water you consume. This is also the same article that says whales have more efficient kidneys than humans and that seabirds have a nose gland to remove salt. So, whatever.

The gull's nose kidney contributes to its haughty disdain for humans. One need spend only a little time around gulls, especially a group, to experience their ongoing insults and gossip about what you're wearing, your hairstyle, and the glands with which you were or were not born. Their foul-mouthed language set back universal translator technology by decades.

~6~
Start a fire.

Some people like their water "boiled," to "kill parasites" and "not develop gastrointestinal issues." To inspire a fire with which to boil water, you might try the create-friction-with-a-stick method, or the flint-and-stone-spark method, or the thick-glasses-to-concentrate-sun method, or the handheld-lighter method, or the just-a-little-gasoline-on-the-charcoal-briquettes method, whatever works best for you.

~7~
Practice shadow puppets.

A benefit of having a fire is the ability to turn hand and body shapes into shadowy rabbits, crocodiles, and other clever representations. Use the firelight to cast representative shadows. Try making a shadow rescue vessel because that would be funny.

If you're unable to start or maintain a fire, color in the
picture and think warm thoughts.

~8~
Fret.

Constantly worry that your fire will go out, and you won't be able to get it started again.

~9~
Build a beacon.

Don't be afraid to ask for help. This is an opportunity to show your personal style. Would you prefer to write a large "SOS" in driftwood on the sand? Perhaps you are more of a "giant pile of flammable material that could be lit upon sighting a vessel" type of person. Whatever you do, make it you!

~10~
Spell check.

Writing words on the beach using sticks or stones won't be effective if would-be rescuers don't understand your message.

~11~
Cultivate.

If your island is both deserted and a desert, consider looking at options to irrigate and grow what crops you can, so that you are able to endure life longer.

Sure, you might be tempted to put off planting because you hope for a swift rescue. Just remember that you can't harvest what you don't cultivate. Well, unless it grows on its own. In that case, it might not need irrigation. But without care, your harvest needs might exceed replacement crop growth. Don't just lounge carelessly on the beach!

This being a general guidebook, it doesn't have specific instructions on how to design an effective irrigation system or what to grow using the system you are able to achieve with your specific island conditions. Instead, it offers you the joy of exploring how to garden, motivated by survival-based fear.

~12~
Scavenge.

Traditionally defined as looking for objects in rubbish, scavenging early for the remnants of the vessel that brought you here can make a difference throughout the duration of your island stay. Plus, it represents a more environmentally responsible approach to being marooned.

Contemplate what you might do with what you find, such as creating whimsical yard art.

~13~
Explore resources.

Get to know the natural wonders around you. What plants might you use to make shelter? What plants might you eat? What plants might you regret eating? What plants might you regret using as toilet paper? Scratch that curiosity itch!

Some plants produce delicious berries that are as easy to access as they are agreeable, while others will nip you with their thorns if you try to take something from them. This is not entirely unlike people. Learn when the reward is worth the risk.

~14~
Dig a latrine.

Everybody poops, but you need not excrete randomly. Plan a strategic hole or, better yet, create a composting toilet. Remember to achieve an optimal composting temperature for your excrement so that it destroys pathogens. Note that you can be more efficient with your potty time if you incorporate a combination metal forge and crafting station. If you decide to design a multifunction toilet, explore what you can do while you're taking a poo.

~15~
Head off trouble.

Covering your head with a wide-brimmed hat can help protect your face from sunburn now and ward off skin cancer later. If you were not stranded with a hat, work on weaving one. Incorporate native flowers, nuts, and fruits.

~16~
Hang a hammock.

Don't have a hammock? You'll need to figure out how to harvest fibrous plants to weave into ropelike lengths of enforced fiber. Combine those strands of fiber in a crosshatch pattern to create a net at least as long as your body. With rope on each end, you can hang it between two trees. Use the net to catch some sleep.

~17~
Learn how to get into and out of a hammock.

~18~
Make a friend.

Literally, look around for materials and craft a companion to keep you company.

~19~
Celebrate your survival.

You've made it this far! What better way to celebrate than by creating a fun or whimsical beverage container out of a coconut?

If your exploration of the island includes discovery of ice and a blender, splurge on a tropical slush. You've earned it!

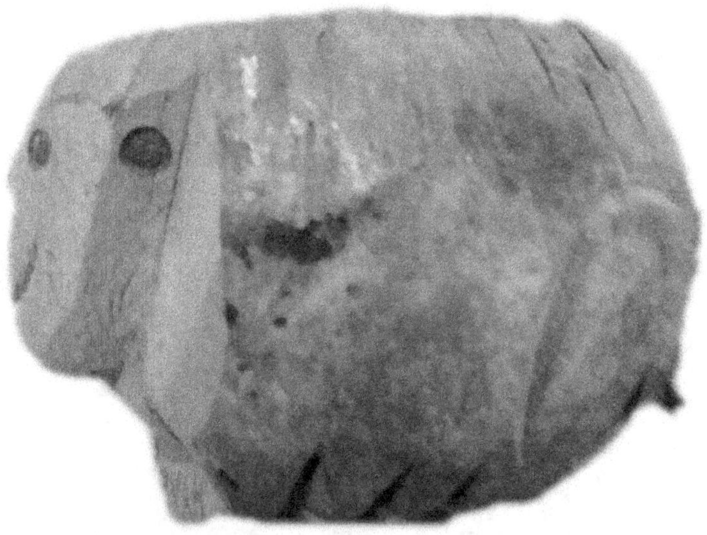

If you carve a face in a coconut beverage container, you will have someone to talk to while you're drinking.

~20~
Go fish.

First, you will need a fishing pole and bait. A net is also helpful. These items may commonly be purchased at a sporting goods store or tackle shop.

~21~
Make a fishing spear.

If you are unable to locate a retail establishment to purchase fishing equipment, try using a sharp stick to stab fish in the water.

~22~
Make a fishing net.

If you find yourself completely inept at stabbing fish with your fishing spear, use plant fiber or salvaged rope to weave a fishing net. Throw the net over the fish and drag them onto land.

~23~
Make a fish trap.

If you are not successful with catching fish in a net or forget to hold onto the end of the net when you throw it, try to weave a fish trap. A funnel fish trap is like a long basket with an inward-pointing, narrowing entrance. Think of a candy jar where someone is going to store small, no-brand-name chocolate candies with a hard candy coating. Placing a funnel on top of the candy jar allows them to pour the bag of generic candies into the jar without spilling. Imagine you want some candies, but the person hasn't taken the funnel away. You squeeze your hand down that funnel and into the delicious pile, but your chocolate-filled fingers don't fit on the way back out. Like you, fish swim down the funnel into the trap, become confused, and they can't swim out before you retrieve the trap. Thus, you help the overall fish population by consuming the ones that can't figure out how to just ask for a candy instead of being prematurely greedy.

~24~
Play Go Fish!

The classic card game Go Fish! involves one player asking another player if they have a card of the same type as one in their hand. The other player must give all they have of that type. Otherwise, the second player proclaims, "Go fish!" and prompts the first player to draw a card from the deck. A player who gets all four cards of a type places them on display. The one with the most four-card sets wins. If you are alone, you can occupy the roles of both first and second players.

~25~
Get away from annoying coworkers.

If you're alone, you don't have to worry about someone stealing your lunch from the break room fridge or talking over you on a virtual conference call.

~26~
Exercise your desire for control.

You know how if you want something done right, you have to do it yourself? Being stranded alone on an island is your opportunity to finally have everything done right, since there's no one around but you to do anything.

~27~
Leverage illness.

Catch a rare disease that causes you to forget your troubles and all the things that made you vulnerable, miserable, obligated, or suspicious of the world.

If you survive, you won't know that you were ever enemies with someone, had a disappointing experience, or learned something that you would have been happier not knowing. This will change your life.

Shells come in an abundance of sizes, shapes, colors, and textures, kind of like people. Their hard exterior protects tender life inside, kind of like people. Incorporating them into your décor can add interest and theme to your surroundings. Shells, that is. Maybe also people.

~28~

Craft a keepsake box.

Turn ordinary seashells into a decorative container for precious mementoes by affixing them to the outside of a wooden box.

First, build a wooden box. Then, affix shells.

~29~
Find mementoes.

Have a keepsake box, but it's empty? Gather knickknacks, tchotchkes, and bric-a-brac to store there. Make sure what you gather will fit into your box. Otherwise, you will have to build a bigger box or just forget about it. Instead of having mementoes, you'll have mementnoes.

~30~
Push a button.

Everyone needs a purpose. Find a button and push it, helping yourself maintain the desire to get out of your hammock in the morning.

~31~
Build a button.

If your deserted island lacks a button, you can make your own.

~32~
Build many buttons.

You might eventually need some new clothes, with all the scampering about you're doing on this island. You now have time to try rock buttons, wood buttons, mushroom buttons. See what works the best. If you develop your practical need into a button passion, you perhaps can look forward to joining the National Button Society and forming new and rewarding friendships once you're rescued.

~33~
Push someone else's button.

If you're fortunate enough to be stranded with someone else or be hallucinating a companion, you have the perfect opportunity to learn how to be as annoying as possible, bringing them to the edge of retribution and then luring them back into friendship and co-dependency.

Author H. G. Wells foresaw the day when your army of enhanced squirrel super-soldiers carries you to victory.

~34~

Craft someone whose buttons you might push.

Secrecy is an advantage of a deserted island.

It provides a location to practice vivisection, the sometimes frowned-upon act of operating on live animals (or humans) for experimentation and scientific research. Have you always wanted to see if you can create the perfect being? Now is your chance, away from prying eyes, until you are ready. As a more modern approach, you might try DNA manipulation or ability-boosting implants.

Just be careful that this torturous endeavor doesn't result in something that wants to do more than push your buttons in return.

~35~
Form a tribe.

You'll need to gather allies if you want to maximize your chances of surviving. Don't forget to come up with a cool name or theme for your group, clan, cadre, coterie, clique, or pack. Deciding on a name, on its own, will take days. If you're all alone, repeat activity #18 as often as necessary.

~36~
Go to war with another tribe.

Where would humanity be without constant war and strife? If these aren't good things, why would we keep doing them? Take advantage of this motivating force to transform your island by exploring inventions, medical response, and trauma psychology.

~37~
Bury a chest of treasure.

Don't have a chest or treasure? Slackers like you must wait for pirates to come along with their treasure.

~38~
Fight pirates for treasure.

Before you face invasion, you will find it helpful to rig a variety of traps around the island and build a hardy tree fort.

A pirate's flag means one of two things: An upcoming epic swashbuckling battle or a family-friendly comic romp. Prepare the appropriate music.

~39~

Lead a mutiny.

Should pirates bring their ship to your island, remember that a person disliking the captain is just a fellow mutineer you haven't met yet. If successful, you and your newly acquired pirate crew can engage with psychologist Bruce Tuckman's model of the stages of team development: forming, storming, norming, and performing. If you reach the adjourning stage, be careful you don't find yourself the target of a mutiny, abandoned on a deserted island.

Bet you're missing toilet paper.

~40~

Catch up on gratitude.

By now, you might be missing all of those things you previously had, from hot running water to grocery stores. Turn that frustration and longing into retroactive gratefulness.

~41~
Plan for gratitude.

Dream about being back in civilization and all that you will appreciate once you are there. Close your eyes and see it in your mind's eye. What does it feel like? How might you express that once you're back? Hoarding toilet paper is a valid response, but what else might you try?

~42~
Befriend local wildlife.

Become acquainted with the types of animals already living on and around your island so that you can make a solid decision about the type of animal you would most like to befriend.

Watch for red flags that the animal may not be a good fit for your friendship, such as trying to maim you.

~43~
Befriend local plant life.

If you land on an island with sentient plants, you would be wise to create a positive relationship. However, it should not be so positive that you allow your body to be taken over and released back to humanity to spread their dire plant plans. Boundaries are important to healthy relationships.

~44~
Befriend local paranormal life.

You might not be the first person to be stranded on this particular deserted island. The ghost of a formerly shipwrecked person could tell you entertaining stories around the fire. Just because someone is dead, it doesn't mean that they can no longer be good company. You might even pick up some tips for when you haunt the next stranded person, so stay curious.

~45~
Invent.

Design deserted island versions of modern amenities, like a pedal-driven clothes washer or a coconut phone. You need not be stranded without a single luxury. You don't have to be a professor to figure out clever solutions, although it does help.

~46~
Craft coconut clothing.

By now, your own clothes might be looking a little ragged, and you've hopefully noticed that coconut shells are durable. Create something to wear that covers body bits you want to keep safe.

Just because coconut shells are hard, like nature's armor, doesn't mean you can't explore softer options with the coir, the husk around the hard inner shell.

~47~
Invent a clothing line.

Don't stop at coconuts when it comes to wearable creations. Grass skirts and the bikini, named after that island, are synonymous with island life. Have you never heard of *sandalls?* Not sandals, with one l, but footwear made entirely out of sand? No? That's because you haven't invented them yet!

Once you get back to civilization, you should have an entire collection of all-natural, survival-inspired designs that will be the talk of the runways.

~48~
Learn to sashay.

If you don't practice your runway moves, how are you going to model your clothing creations and wow them during Fashion Week?

When your place on the beach requires maintenance, it may be time you risked life and limb to explore the heights and depths for a possible second home.

~49~
Spelunk.

Your island might have an exciting and beautiful sea cave or a cavern high on the mountain with a distant view, unreachable by even a tall, toothy Tyrannosaurus rex. Why avoid these intriguing places, just because you're alone and could be seriously injured without even the potential of someone helping you? Just don't fall or get caught by the incoming tide. Easy.

~50~
Gather gems.

Keep your eye out for fabulous wealth that has previously gone unnoticed. Collecting gems, even uncut ones, will allow you to go home rich. So what if you might end up spending the rest of your days lamenting what you cannot buy with the pretty stones you've collected because your island has no stores.

~51~
Plot revenge.

Let's face it: It's somebody's fault you're here. It is most certainly not your fault. Relish those long hours dreaming of how you'll get even once you're away from this place. Wallow in the emotion. Revisit again and again the memories of what lead up to the unfortunate event and why, precisely, it is the fault of your chosen blame target.

~52~
Craft paper.

Learn to pulp vegetation fiber, strain out the water and spread the results to dry, eventually increasing the quality of your creation until it matches high-end stationery that no one would buy anyway because people just don't write letters like they used to. Realize an unfair stationery assumption distracted you. Appreciate your handcrafted paper. Scent it.

~53~
Create a diary.

Chronicle your struggles on this island. Capture your triumphs and troubles, your regrets and realizations.

Document all of the things that make you vulnerable, miserable, obligated, or suspicious of the world so that, should you catch a rare disease that causes you to forget your troubles, you can reconnect with them in your own writing and appreciate the lessons those experiences brought you. Consider the idea that lessons from experiences are filtered through choices and perspectives we can control.

Keep your journal with you at all times so that you don't miss any opportunities to record an insight. Plan to capture the moment of your death with an incomplete sentence to taunt whoever finds it, as a final salute to the mysteries of the universe and human psyche.

~54~
Write to your future self.

A letter to yourself that you read in 10 years can provide helpful insight that can enrich your future.

Reading it will also give you something to do if you're still on the island.

~55~
Write letters to your loved ones.

If something untoward should happen to you, wouldn't you want those you care about to know your deepest thoughts about them?

~56~
Write letters to your enemies.

If something untoward should happen to you, wouldn't you want those you despise to know your deepest thoughts about them?

The same moon that shines on you also shines on those you love, so far away. And on those you hate, so far away. Unless the person you love and/or hate is yourself, then not so far away.

~57~
List-build.

Create a list of 1,001 things to experience before you die.

~58~
Make progress.

Cross "struggle to survive on a deserted island" off of your list of 1,001 things to experience before you die.

~59~
Write a will.

Maybe you created a will before you traveled or experienced whatever happened that lead to you being stuck on this island. By now, the heirs have probably divided up your stuff — at least the stuff they know about. But who will inherit your invaluable island clothing line designs?

~60~
Stay positive.

Studies show that an optimistic attitude contributes to successful endeavors.

Smile, though your leg is breaking from falling out of a coconut tree.

Laugh, though all the fish outsmarted your trap, and your kelp-powered refrigerator broke a thousand miles from the nearest repair shop.

Hope, though your *sandalls* fell apart when you were walking across prickly plants you thought you could trust, and now their poisonous barbs are lodged in your feet, causing intense itching and swelling.

Flip through this book. Do you see "Give up" as one of the 101 things to do on a deserted island? No, you do not! It might be in the sequel, but it is not here!

~61~
Succeed.

Most people struggle with uncertainty and a loss of confidence sometimes. When you're trying to do a hard thing, you might forget to acknowledge the effort it requires of you just to stay alive, let alone accomplish larger goals. You could benefit from a little boost, a win, an accomplishment just for the sake of feeling success. Climb to the highest point on the island, just to say you've done it. Plant your flag to celebrate.

~62~
Design a flag.

If climbing to the top of the island made you realize you lack a personal flag, spend some time contemplating what flag design truly represents you and your unique brand. Flag in hand, decide if you want to climb to the top again or if you'll just plant it in your garden.

Even if you're just a beginning painter, you could create
your own version of this thrilling, vibrant sunset.
Embrace the doing, not just the end product.

~63~
Capture the view.

Sure, you might be able to take a photographic selfie, but what happens when your battery dies? Turn to painting!

By carrying your easel with you wherever you go, you'll be able to quickly work on an image of a sunset, a forest scene, or a wild animal stalking you.

~64~
Confirm that you are not actually in a video game.

A fair number of video games take place on islands. Why not your island? How would you know if you were or were not merely in a game? Spend some time working through this reality challenge. For instance, you might try bludgeoning down a tree with your fists. Do you ever feel like you have leveled up?

~65~
Embrace your mythic quest.

It may be that you were stranded on this island as part of a feud involving ancient gods, nymphs, cyclopes, giants, or your parental figures. Keep an eye out for signs, such as caves full of free food, bags filled with various winds, and beings with the ability to turn others into sheep. Once you know you have a quest, don't be stereotypical and try to avoid answering the call. We all know that you're going to be forced to embrace your destiny in the end. Stop pussyfooting around about it.

~66~
Decide on a likeness.

Famous islands typically are shaped like something, such as a skull, an elephant, or a fish. This imagery will help you later, when you're sharing the story of being stranded on a deserted island.

~67~
Name your island.

Come on! You've been here all this time, and you don't even know your island's name? What kind of a relationship is that?! Have you considered asking your island what it would like to be called? Have you even tried out a name, perhaps based on its shape? You might name it after yourself, something like Island of the Lost YourName or YourFirstName's Doom?

~68~
Build a monument.

Pick a highly visible place on your island and construct something to commemorate your time here. A statue of yourself, for example. In the future, visitors will be able to tour ruins of your monument to yourself and remember you. Perhaps as a bit egotistical, but still remembered.

~69~
Develop a tourist attraction.

You must not give up on connecting with civilization, no matter how long you languish alone, all alone, with no one. Millions of people each year visit theme parks, pay for guided tours, and sign up for all-inclusive resorts. With so many people drawn to your unique and exciting destination, you might be able to hitch a ride home with them when they leave.

~70~
Hitch a ride.

Is your island home to a large bird, flying reptile, or other creature capable of carrying your weight and navigating you to civilization? You're in luck! Build a saddle or sling, climb up to its nest, or wherever it spends its leisure time, and revel in your view as you take to the skies.

Imagine soaring above and between islands on a living creature or a smoky monster, whichever you connect with best. Be sure to develop some way to steer your friend, or you may end up on an entirely different island, still stranded.

~72~
Learn a musical instrument.

Expressing yourself through music stirs the soul in ways that meet a deep need unfulfilled by words alone.

Whether it's clopping two halves of coconuts together or blowing on a reed whistle, you can learn to perform your own version of "Free Bird."

~71~
Mosh.

A style of wild dancing that involves colliding with others, mosh is also referred to as slam dancing. Places where mosh happens are called mosh pits, and they are sometimes prohibited because they're seen as too violent. With no one else to hurt, feel free to dig a pit and bounce around in it, without authoritative restriction.

~73~
Connect with the local population.

Upon exploration, you might discover that your island is not actually deserted. You would not be the first with this experience. Be they 6 inches or 600 inches tall (15.24 centimeters or 1,524 centimeters), you will find that societies the world over have their own customs, joys, and challenges. You might experiment with offering your perspective or guidance and see what that gets you.

~74~
Learn another system of measurement.

You have time to learn how others measure.

Here's a start:
1 inch = 2.54 centimeters
1 mile = 160,934 centimeters
1 liter = 33.814 U.S. fluid ounces

~75~
Have a spa day.

The struggle to survive can be tough. Don't you deserve some "me time?" Seaweed facial, hot stone massage, trim and polish those dirty, dirty nails.

"My infrared sauna experience gave me a new outlook on life."

—reincarnated tourist, Isle of the Dead

~76~
Swim with marine creatures.

Vacationers pay good money to swim with dolphins, sea turtles, and sharks. Fortunately, you can do it without having to pay anyone, not even a sand dollar.

It may seem like a starfish wants to give you a high five,
but don't trust these water-dwelling fiends. The first
chance they get, they'll attach to your face and try to suck
out your brain.

~77~

Contemplate the meaning of life.

Why did this happen? Why did this happen to you? Is there some grand plan that involves you experiencing a stranding now? To what extent did you control whether or not this happened to you? Is there some greater power at work in your life? In the world? In the universe? If so, what does that mean about history and current events? You might find peace, or you might lose your grip on reality.

~78~

Find the mad scientist's lair.

You could be sharing the island with a secret lair. If the island has a volcano, the hideout is likely located near there. At the lair, you might find a way off via submarine, helicopter, unidentified flying machine, or teleportation device. You might also save the world in the process!

~79~
Become a mad scientist.

Some start with science and get an island lair. You could start with an island and develop from there.

~80~
Befriend a Brachiosaurus.

If your island includes a thriving culture built around friendship with talking dinosaurs, take advantage of the opportunity to create a real connection.

Remember that dinosaur watercolor you did as a child? Imagine it coming to life, with more definition and skin.

~81~
Conquer a cadre of Compsognathus.

If your island's dinosaurs are not particularly friendly, draw on your wits, skill, and tenacity to stay safe. A compy* may look cute, but a welcome party with those little fellas can ruin your day.

*Don't get distracted by the wildly popular barroom debate about the chicken-sized Jurassic-era skeleton of the *Compsognathus longipes* found in Bavaria as compared to the use of a venomous *Procompsognathus* in popular culture. That's how brawls start.

~82~
Tame a wild stallion.

Ride along the beach on your beautiful, black stallion as your hair flows behind you in the wind.

~83~
Zipline.

You'll get around the island faster by gliding through the trees using a grooved pulley on a line. Watch out for the branches!

~84~

Start a library.

Rescuers, pirates, or others who join you in your stranding might enjoy reading your thoughts about island life, your adventures, and the role of leadership in a survival setting. Be sure to set up a system whereby they can check out books and return them, as appropriate.

Remember that libraries offer more than books. Consider expanding your collection to a "library of things" that can be checked out, such as a hoe, a bucket and shovel for sandcastle building, or a tiny iguana saddle and top hat.

~85~
Welcome guests.

If you were stranded here while you were minding your own business, chances are others might fall victim to the same quirk of fate. Offer tea.

~86~
Delegate.

Incorporate others stranded into an organized cooperative so that you can more effectively survive together.

~87~
Compensate equitably.

Decide how you should all be rewarded for your contributions to the group's success. Maybe you should get a bigger share because you've been here longer?

~88~
Alienate coinhabitants.

Nobody's perfect, not even you. Maybe it's your know-it-all attitude from having been on this island for so long, or maybe it's your fear of being abandoned again that makes you clingy and/or obnoxious. Embrace the sensation of driving others to despise you.

~89~
Wallow in regret.

There is only so much someone can take. The time will come when you need to get away from the crowd, perhaps to accomplish some task no one else has bothered to finish that you have to head off alone to do, with a heavy sigh. When the late-coming survivors are rescued while you are on the other side of the island, and they are so upset with you that they don't tell the rescuers you're around, take this opportunity for self-reflection.

~90~
Build a raft.

You may eventually succumb to the lure of trying to rescue yourself, despite your trepidation about trying to sail the open seas on a floating structure that you built. You might be less concerned about venturing forth in a raft designed for survival at sea, but for the sake of this book, you don't have that. Nope. Nary an inflatable in sight.

You may as well get started by picking out a name for your raft. Strive to live up to the vision of your raft's name. Floaty McDucky owes you for its existence.

~91~
Gather sailing supplies.

It isn't enough just to own a raft. You'll need food, water, a means of keeping the weather off of you, and party music.

~92~
Practice your interview pose.

If you ever make it back to civilization, what sort of image do you want to project? Teach your face to express relief, concern, humility, and admirable courage so that you can summon those looks on demand for adoring media and fans.

Practice posing with your raft, demonstrating how you built the raft, looking windswept and sea-washed, and voguing.

~93~
Trash your raft.

Try to be creative with this one. Barrier reefs, wrathful octopi, dolphin gangs, and poor construction are some common options for why you end up clinging to the wreckage and washing back ashore, barely alive but with a heightened appreciation for life.

While you might want to enjoy some rock music on your raft, you don't want to jam your raft onto rocks.

~94~
Create an escape plan.

Deep down, you knew that raft wasn't going to get you where you wanted, didn't you? You can hide the truth from others but not from the sea. Take time to carefully develop a plan to escape your island, preferably one that doesn't involve a poorly constructed raft. Scoff at your prior raft efforts and realize that failure to plan really is planning to fail. Do better.

~95~
Read a listicle about reasons escape plans fail.

Top 5 Reasons Escape Plans Fail
1. Plan fails to account for all factors.
2. Lack of resources.
3. Lack of follow-through.
4. Unrealistic expectations.
5. Human error.

~96~
Scoff.

Spend time mocking the listicle, questioning its validity, noting that it doesn't have an expert source associated with it.

Of course you have lack of resources! If you had resources, you could just escape on your own private yacht, piloted by someone with an interesting accent. Your yacht crew would be ready with a chilled beverage and your favorite nosh. Ridiculous listicle.

That sort of thing. Really get that contempt going.

~97~
Create an escape plan B.

Failure is just a step along the way to success. Learn from your mistakes and the wisdom of the listicle. Create a plan B.

~98~
Implement escape plan B.

Having the courage to get up and try again is its own skill, one that will serve you well if you ever return to civilization. Think the plan out, yes, but don't let thinking prevent trying.

~99~
Improvise.

Escape efforts might generate new and unexpected dangers, such as encountering icebergs or a storm, a container leak leading to a lack of potable water on the open ocean, or crashing into the giant leg of an ancient god who is standing in the cove. You'll need to stay alert to respond to each crisis. Failing multiple times doesn't make you a failure, necessarily. Your most important resources are your wits and your plucky will to keep trying, even when it seems pretty obvious that you're just not up to this challenge.

Orcas have been called "killer whales," but they're actually like watery panda bears. If you encounter any, encourage them to get up onto your raft for cuddles.

~100~
Create a really good escape plan, grounded in knowledge.

Time for the rubber to meet the road, right?

Get that train out of the station. Mail the letter. Lace up the shoes. Slide the pizza in the oven.

Recall all of the time you spent researching how to escape a deserted island, from online first-person testimonial videos to lengthy articles with diagrams.* Remember the adage that failure to plan is planning to fail. Scowl at said adage. You didn't fail to plan. You are bringing to your efforts the power of knowledge, a significant ally.

*If you failed to do any research before becoming stranded, you might skip this thing to do and instead spend the time and effort wishing you had found the time. Let this be a lesson to you!

Whether your island is real or metaphoric, let your experiences and choices transform you into the winged creature you've always had the potential to be, however deep inside. Create contentment in your island home, or grow your own wings and fly to a better place.

~101~
Become an improved person.

Let your circumstances help you embrace new experiences, laugh a little more, love a little better, and appreciate what you've got. Such as this book. <u>Such as this book.</u> *Where might you have been without this book?*